MICHAEL HAGUE'S

TREASURED CLASSICS

chronicle books · san francisco

Library of Congress Cataloging-in-Publication Data
Hague, Michael.
Michael Hague's treasured classics / written and illustrated by
Michael Hague.
p. cm.
Contents: Chicken-Licken—Cinderella—Goldilocks and the three
bears—Jack and the beanstalk—Little Red Riding-Hood—The
elves and the shoemaker—The gingerbread man—The grasshopper
and the ant—The princess and the pea—The Sleeping Beauty—
The three billy goats gruff—The three little pigs—The tortoise and
the hare—The ugly duckling.
ISBN 978-0-8118-4904-3
1. Fairy tales. 2. Tales. [1. Fairy tales. 2. Folklore.] I. Title.
PZ8.H1253Tr 2011
398.2—dc22
[E]
2010008551

Book design by Natalie Davis.
Typeset in Janson Text.
The illustrations in this book were rendered in pencil and
digitally painted.

Manufactured by Toppan Leefung, Da Ling Shan Town,
Dongguan, China, in July 2011.

MIX
Paper from
responsible sources
FSC® C104723

10 9 8 7 6 5 4 3 2 1

This product conforms to CPSIA 2008.

Chronicle Books LLC
680 Second Street, San Francisco, California 94107

www.chroniclekids.com

For Bixby and Van

THE STORY OF
CHICKEN-LICKEN

One day Chicken-Licken was scratching for food when an acorn dropped out of a tree and hit her on the head. "Goodness gracious me!" squawked Chicken-Licken, "the sky is falling; I must go and tell the king."

So she ran along until she met Henny-Penny.

"Where are you going, Chicken-Licken?" asked Henny-Penny.

"Oh! Henny-Penny, the sky is falling and I'm going to tell the king."

"How do you know the sky is falling?" asked Henny-Penny.

"A piece of it fell on my head!" cried Chicken-Licken.

"Then we must hurry and tell the king," clucked Henny-Penny.

So Chicken-Licken and Henny-Penny ran along until they met Cocky-Locky.

"Where are you going?" asked Cocky-Locky.

"Oh! Cocky-Locky, the sky is falling and we are going to tell the king," replied Henny-Penny.

"How do you know the sky is falling?" asked Cocky-Locky.

"A piece of it fell on my head!" cried Chicken-Licken.

"Then we must hurry and tell the king," crowed Cocky-Locky.

So Chicken-Licken, Henny-Penny, and Cocky-Locky ran along until they met Ducky-Lucky.

"Where are you going?" asked Ducky-Lucky.

"Oh! Ducky-Lucky, the sky is falling and we are going to tell the king," replied Cocky-Locky.

"How do you know the sky is falling?" asked Ducky-Lucky.

"A piece of it fell on my head!" cried Chicken-Licken.

"Then we must hurry and tell the king," quacked Ducky-Lucky.

So Chicken-Licken, Henny-Penny, Cocky-Locky, and Ducky-Lucky ran along until they met Goosey-Loosey.

"Where are you going?" asked Goosey-Loosey.

"Oh! Goosey-Loosey, the sky is falling and we are going to tell the king," replied Ducky-Lucky.

"How do you know the sky is falling?" asked Goosey-Loosey.

"A piece of it fell on my head!" cried Chicken-Licken.

"Then we must hurry and tell the king," honked Goosey-Loosey.

So Chicken-Licken, Henny-Penny, Cocky-Locky, Ducky-Lucky, and Goosey-Loosey ran along until they met Turkey-Lurkey.

"Where are you going?" asked Turkey-Lurkey.

"Oh! Turkey-Lurkey, the sky is falling and we are going to tell the king," replied Goosey-Loosey.

"How do you know the sky is falling?" asked Turkey-Lurkey.

"A piece of it fell on my head!" cried Chicken-Licken.

"Then we must hurry and tell the king," gobbled Turkey-Lurkey.

So Chicken-Licken, Henny-Penny, Cocky-Locky, Ducky-Lucky, Goosey-Loosey, and Turkey-Lurkey ran along until they met Foxy-Woxy.

"Where are you going, Chicken-Licken, Henny-Penny, Cocky-Locky, Ducky-Lucky, Goosey-Loosey, and Turkey-Lurkey?" asked Foxy-Woxy.

"Oh! Foxy-Woxy, the sky is falling and we are going to tell the king," replied Turkey-Lurkey.

"How do you know the sky is falling?" asked Foxy-Woxy.

"A piece of it fell on my head!" cried Chicken-Licken.

"Then we must hurry and tell the king," growled Foxy-Woxy. "Follow me and I shall show you a shortcut."

So Chicken-Licken, Henny-Penny, Cocky-Locky, Ducky-Lucky, Goosey-Loosey, and Turkey-Lurkey followed Foxy-Woxy. They came to a dark, narrow hole that looked suspiciously like the door to Foxy-Woxy's cave. "Don't worry," said Foxy-Woxy. "This is the shortcut to the king's palace. You'll get there quickly if you follow me."

So Chicken-Licken, Henny-Penny, Cocky-Locky, Ducky-Lucky, Goosey-Loosey, and Turkey-Lurkey followed Foxy-Woxy into his dark cave. Once inside, Foxy-Woxy snapped quickly at Chicken-Licken, but he ended up with only a mouth full of feathers.

"Oh!"cried Chicken-Licken. "Run, Run, RUN!"

So Turkey-Lurkey, Goosey-Loosey, Ducky-Lucky, Cocky-Locky, Henny-Penny, and Chicken-Licken turned tail and did not stop running until they reached home, and the king was never told that the sky was falling.

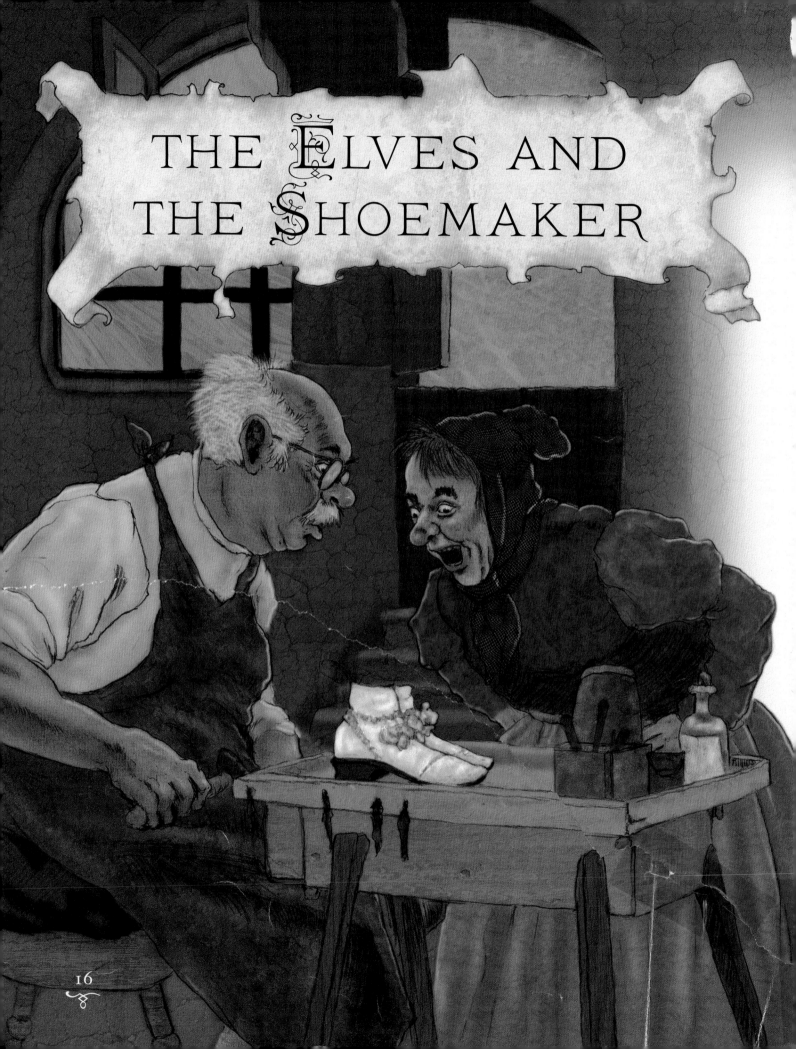

THE ELVES AND THE SHOEMAKER

Once upon a time there was a shoemaker and his good wife who, through no fault of their own, had become so poor that the shoemaker found himself with just enough leather left to make one last pair of shoes. Before going to bed, he cut out the leather so that first thing the next morning he could begin work. Then, with a good conscience, the shoemaker and his wife said their prayers and went to sleep.

In the morning when the shoemaker sat down to work, to his surprise, he found the pair of shoes standing finished on his table. He was amazed. He took the shoes in his hand to examine them more closely. They were neatly sewn; not a stitch was out of place. A finer piece of work he had never seen.

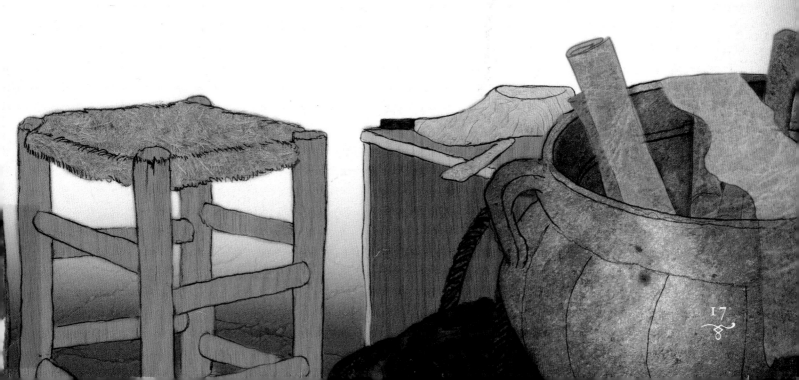

The shoemaker put the shoes in his store window. Soon a customer saw them and because they were of such wonderful quality paid more than the usual price. With the money he had gotten for the shoes, the shoemaker was able to buy enough leather to make two pairs of shoes.

As before, he cut them out in the evening and in the morning, much to his surprise, the shoes were finished. He had no sooner placed the shoes in the window when two customers arrived and paid liberally for the wonderful shoes. These gave him so much money that he was now able to buy leather for four pairs of shoes.

The next morning he found the four pairs finished, and so it continued day after day.

One evening, when the shoemaker had cut out shoes as usual, he said to his wife, "Let's sit up tonight to see who it is that helps us so kindly." The wife agreed, lit a candle, and they hid themselves in the corner of the room.

At midnight, much to their surprise, came a group of little men who crept into the shoemaker's shop, sat down at his table, took up the cut leather, and began to work. Their tiny fingers stitched, sewed, and hammered so neatly and quickly that the shoemaker and his wife could not believe their eyes. Then, when everything was finished, the little helpers ran swiftly away.

The wife said to her husband, "The little men have made us rich, and we must show our gratitude. They run about with barely anything on and must be cold. I will make them little shirts, coats, pants, and warm socks and hats, and you shall make them each a pair of shoes."

The husband agreed and when everything was ready, they laid out the presents on the table instead of the usual work. They hid themselves and waited for the little men to arrive.

At midnight the little men appeared and were about to set to work, but instead of the cut-out leather, they found the tiny clothes. They were delighted. In the twinkling of an eye, they dressed themselves and danced and capered and sprang about, as merry as could be, till at last they danced out the door.

After that, the shoemaker and his good wife saw the little men no more, but they continued to make fine shoes and lived happily to the end of their days.

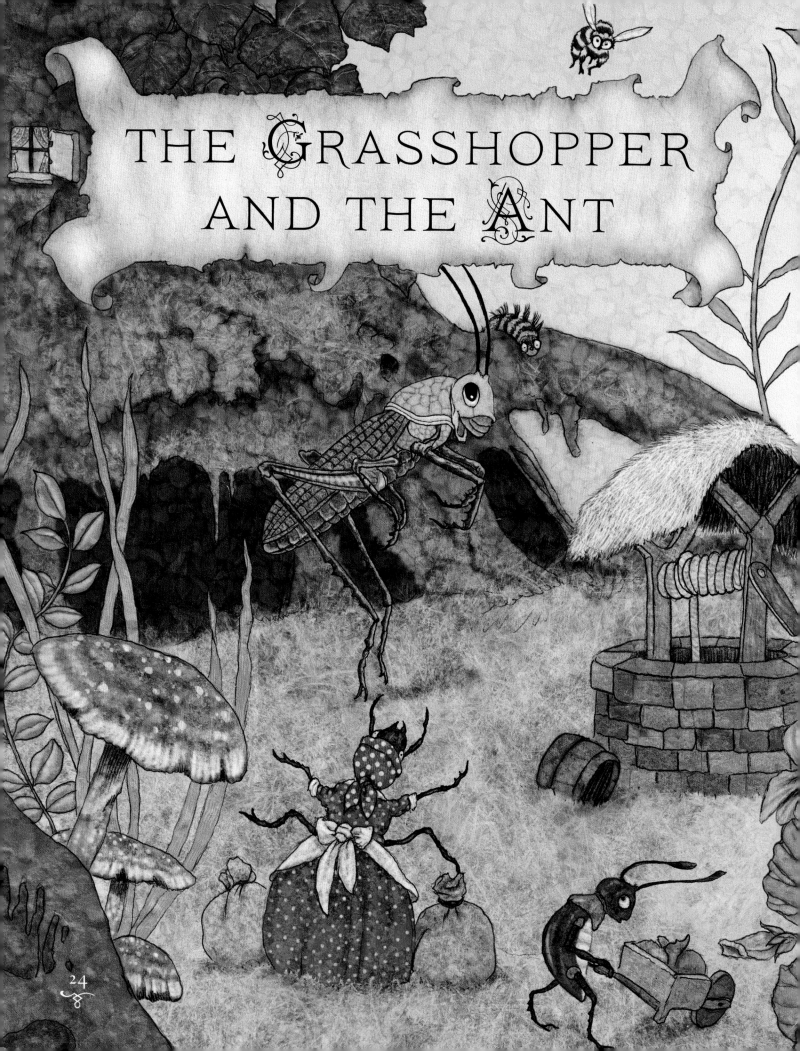

THE GRASSHOPPER AND THE ANT

One perfect summer's day a grasshopper was dancing about, chirping, singing, and playing to his heart's content in the warm sunshine. An ant passed by lugging a sack of grain.

"Hello, Ant," said the grasshopper. "What a fine summer's day it is. Come play in the sunshine instead of toiling away."

"I'm storing food for the winter," said the ant, "and I recommend that you do the same."

The grasshopper laughed. "You collect more food than you can possibly eat! The world is plentiful, dear Ant! Do not be so greedy! Come dance with me. Enjoy your life."

The ant, tired from her work, nonetheless shook her head and kept at her task. "I'm working," she said. "There will be plenty of time to sing and dance when the chores are finished."

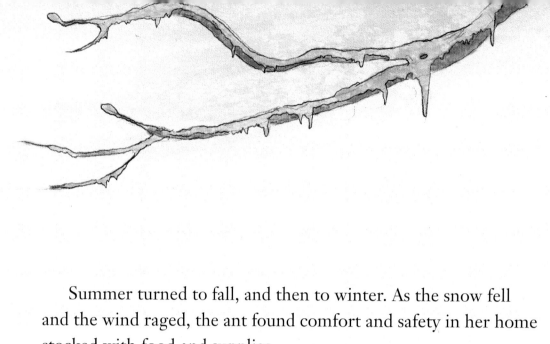

Summer turned to fall, and then to winter. As the snow fell and the wind raged, the ant found comfort and safety in her home stocked with food and supplies.

One stormy day, a knock came at her door. When she opened it, the ant found the grasshopper, half starved and freezing.

"My dear friend," begged the grasshopper. "Please give me some food and shelter!"

The ant replied, "Grasshopper, I worked very hard all summer long and gathered enough supplies to feed and shelter myself for the winter. What did you do all summer long?"

To this the once-merry grasshopper replied, "I sang and danced and played, all through the days and into the nights! It was a wonderful time!"

The ant shook her head and asked, "If it was so enjoyable, why are you not dancing and playing now?"

The grasshopper, shivering and weak, cried, "I cannot! I am too cold and hungry. Have mercy, dear Ant! I will repay you in kind tenfold this summer."

27

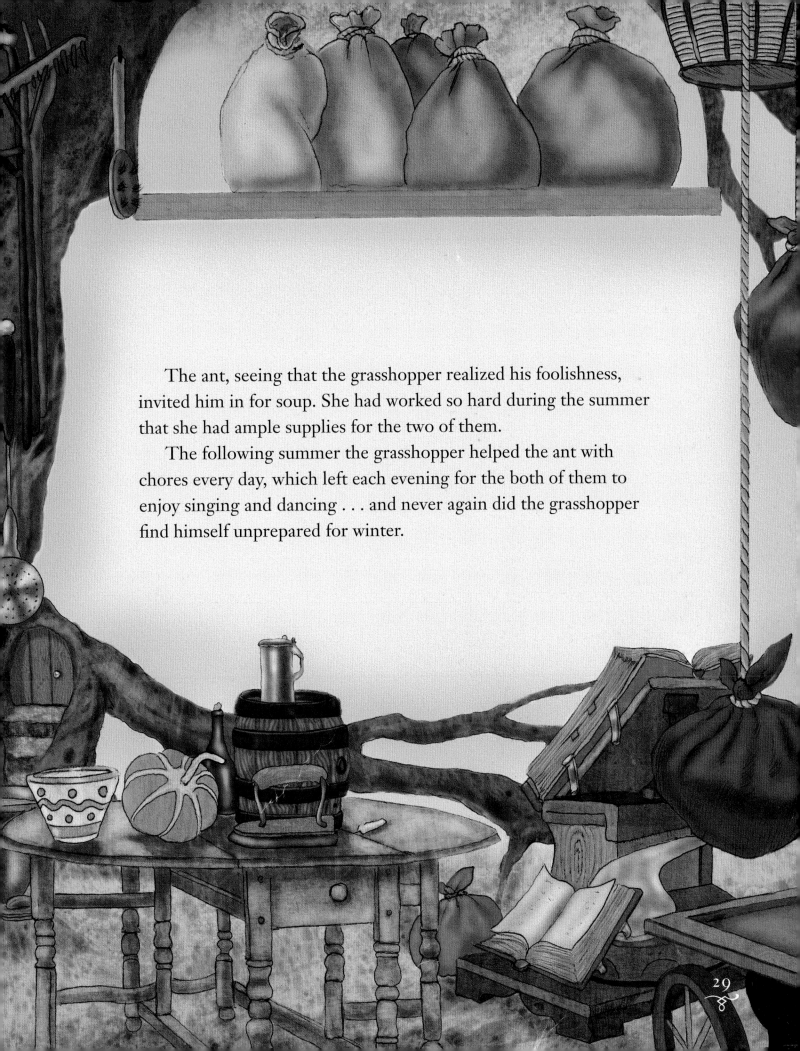

The ant, seeing that the grasshopper realized his foolishness, invited him in for soup. She had worked so hard during the summer that she had ample supplies for the two of them.

The following summer the grasshopper helped the ant with chores every day, which left each evening for the both of them to enjoy singing and dancing . . . and never again did the grasshopper find himself unprepared for winter.

THE SLEEPING BEAUTY

Long ago there lived a king and queen who had no children, although they wanted a child very much. One day, when the queen was walking along the riverbank, she saw a fish lying on the bank, gasping for breath. She took pity on the poor creature and gently put him back into the river. Before he swam away, he told the queen that, in return for her kindness, her dearest wish would come true. And soon thereafter, as the fish had promised, the queen and king at last had a child, a little daughter.

The king and queen held a splendid feast to celebrate the birth of the new princess. They invited kinsfolk, friends, and acquaintances. It was not unusual for there to be fairies in the kingdoms of the world, and they too were invited to the castle.

As was the custom, each fairy gave a special gift to the princess. The first fairy promised her beauty of face and heart; the next, wit and humor; the third, grace and virtue; the fourth, intelligence and the love of learning; the fifth, the gift of music and dance.

The sixth fairy had just stepped forward to offer her gift when she was interrupted by a great noise—and suddenly a very old fairy appeared. She had not been invited because she had not been seen for more than a hundred years and was believed to be dead. Shaking with anger, the old fairy said that the princess would pierce her hand with a spindle on her fifteenth birthday and fall down dead. Then, having taken her revenge for not being invited, she flew away.

The king and queen were in despair. Even the little princess cried at the sad fate gifted to her by the old fairy. But then the sixth fairy stepped forward and said that though she could not undo the evil wish, she could soften the evil spell: her gift was that, when the spindle wounded the princess, she would not die but fall asleep for one hundred years and be awoken by the kiss of her one true prince.

The king, however, hoping to avoid misfortune altogether, proclaimed that all the spinning wheels in the kingdom must be destroyed.

As the years passed, each of the kind fairies' gifts were fulfilled. By her fifteenth year, the princess was so beautiful and wise that she was loved by the entire kingdom. On her fifteenth birthday, the princess had a wonderful party. When it was over, she kissed her parents goodnight and was escorted by her attendants to her bedchamber.

Just as she was about to climb into bed, there was a gentle tapping at the princess's door. Thinking it was one of her attendants, she opened the door but discovered no one there; instead a lovely light sparkled in the hall and floated down the corridor. The princess thought it was a fairy and followed the light through the palace until at last she came to a little tower. She watched as the light disappeared up the stairs and through a door. The princess climbed the stairs, opened the door, and stepped inside. She discovered a small chamber, sparsely furnished with only a small silk-covered couch, and an old woman sitting busily at her work.

The old woman was spinning. The princess had never seen a spinning wheel and was full of curiosity. She asked the old woman what she was doing. The old woman told the princess that she was spinning and showed her how quickly the wheel turned to make the thread. The thread seemed to glow as it was spun. The princess watched for several minutes and then asked if she might try. The old woman bowed to the princess and stepped aside. No sooner had the princess taken the spindle in her hands than the evil fairy's prophecy was fulfilled. The old woman disappeared in a deafening clash of thunder and lightning, and the princess collapsed and fell into a deep sleep.

In moments, the spell touched everyone in the castle. The king and queen and all their court fell asleep. The horses in the stables, the birds in the trees, the cats and dogs, and even the fires in the hearths fell under the spell. A large hedge soon grew around the castle, and year after year it became higher and thicker so that at last the old castle was completely hidden. The old people of the kingdom died, and their children grew up and died as well, as did their children's children, and the story of the Sleeping Beauty became a legend handed down from generation to generation for a hundred years.

On the very day that one hundred years had passed, a prince, both brave and kind, came to the wall that had grown around the castle. He had been told the legend of the Sleeping Beauty by his grandfather and was traveling through the land searching for the enchanted castle. As the prince pushed his way through the thicket, the branches yielded readily to his touch. Thorns fell away and roses bloomed in their place. Primroses sprang up before him and made a path that led him to the castle gates. The prince crossed the courtyard where everyone and everything lay asleep. He entered the castle and passed through rooms full of gentlemen and ladies, all asleep. He walked from hall to hall and climbed stair after stair until at last he reached the tower chamber where the sleeping princess lay. He gazed in wonder at her lovely face and, as fate decreed, the prince kissed the Sleeping Beauty.

At that moment, the spell was broken. The king and queen and all their court awoke. The horses in the stables neighed and shook their glossy manes; the birds broke into song; the cats and dogs stretched their shaggy backs; and the fires in the hearths burned again brightly.

Soon thereafter, the prince and the princess were married and lived happily ever after.

Jack and the Beanstalk

Once upon a time, in a small English village, there lived a poor widow who had an only child named Jack. She loved her son very much, providing for him as best she could. But they became so poor that she did not know how they were going to buy food.

"We must sell our cow," she said one morning. "It is the only thing that we have left."

She told Jack to take the cow and sell it in the next village. Along the way, he met a butcher, who asked him where he was going. When Jack replied that he wished to sell his cow, the butcher offered a bag of lovely colored beans in exchange. He told Jack that the beans were not ordinary beans; they were magic beans.

The silly boy eagerly accepted the offer, gave the cow to the butcher, and returned home excited to show his mother the bag of magic beans. When his mother heard what he had done, she was very angry. She took the beans and threw them out the window. Then, having nothing to eat, they both went supperless to bed.

When Jack awoke the next morning, he discovered that the beans had taken root and sprung up during the night. Their stalks had grown so thick and entwined that they formed a ladder, which disappeared into the clouds.

Curious, Jack decided to climb the beanstalk. His mother came running from the cottage and begged him to come down, but Jack continued up the stalk.

After climbing for some time, Jack broke through the clouds and found himself in a strange land. He left the beanstalk to explore. As he did so, he met a fairy who asked who he was and how he had come to be there. Jack told her how his poor mother had been forced to sell their cow and about the foolish trade he had made for the bag of beans.

The fairy told Jack she had known his father. Jack knew nothing of his father and was eager to hear about him.

"I will tell you all about him," said the fairy. "But first you must agree to do me a favor."

Jack promised to do whatever she requested.

The fairy told Jack that his father had been a rich man, known far and wide for his goodness and generosity. "He never let a day pass without doing a kindness for some person," she said. "It was the wicked giant who destroyed him and his home and took all his wealth. You and your mother barely escaped.

"This giant has killed and eaten a great number of people. Though you will face great dangers, it is your duty to destroy him," the fairy continued. "You must be brave. The giant's castle is north along this road. Take anything the giant has, for it really belongs to you and your mother." Then the fairy disappeared.

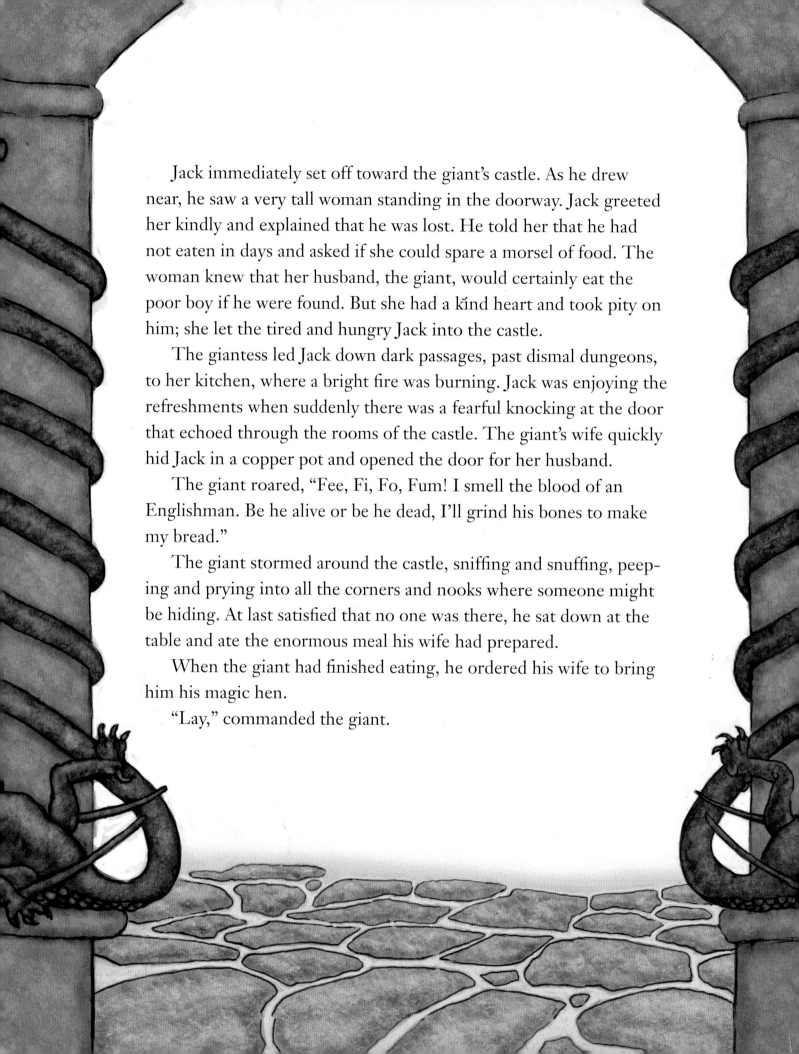

Jack immediately set off toward the giant's castle. As he drew near, he saw a very tall woman standing in the doorway. Jack greeted her kindly and explained that he was lost. He told her that he had not eaten in days and asked if she could spare a morsel of food. The woman knew that her husband, the giant, would certainly eat the poor boy if he were found. But she had a kind heart and took pity on him; she let the tired and hungry Jack into the castle.

The giantess led Jack down dark passages, past dismal dungeons, to her kitchen, where a bright fire was burning. Jack was enjoying the refreshments when suddenly there was a fearful knocking at the door that echoed through the rooms of the castle. The giant's wife quickly hid Jack in a copper pot and opened the door for her husband.

The giant roared, "Fee, Fi, Fo, Fum! I smell the blood of an Englishman. Be he alive or be he dead, I'll grind his bones to make my bread."

The giant stormed around the castle, sniffing and snuffing, peeping and prying into all the corners and nooks where someone might be hiding. At last satisfied that no one was there, he sat down at the table and ate the enormous meal his wife had prepared.

When the giant had finished eating, he ordered his wife to bring him his magic hen.

"Lay," commanded the giant.

Jack peeked out from the copper pot and was amazed to see the hen lay eggs of solid gold.

Soon the giant and his wife fell asleep, and Jack climbed quietly out of the pot. He snatched up the magic hen and did not stop running until he reached the beanstalk. He climbed down and returned home. His mother welcomed him with tears of joy. The golden eggs from the magic hen would provide them with everything they needed and more.

But Jack, intent on keeping his promise to the fairy, climbed the beanstalk the very next day and returned to the giant's castle. Once again, the kindhearted giantess invited Jack in. She warned Jack that he must leave before her husband came home, but the giant returned home earlier than expected. The wife had just enough time to quickly hide Jack inside the copper pot again.

"Fee, Fi, Fo, Fum," roared the giant. "I smell the blood of an Englishman. Be he alive or be he dead, I'll grind his bones to make my bread." The giant was certain that he was not mistaken this time. He searched the castle, sniffing and snuffing, peeping and prying into all the corners and nooks where someone might be hiding. Fortunately for Jack, he did not look inside the copper pot. The giant's wife placed a larger pot of soup on the table, and the giant again decided that it must have been his dinner he had smelled.

After the giant had eaten, he told his wife to bring his bags of gold. The giant grew tired counting the money, and he and his wife soon fell asleep. Jack seized the bags and rushed from the castle. Climbing carefully down the beanstalk, Jack safely reached his home once more.

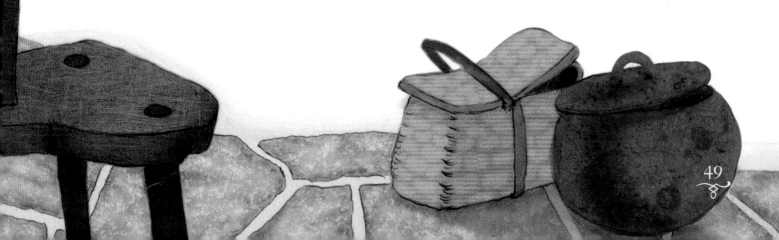

While Jack did not want to worry his mother, he knew he had to keep his promise, and so the very next day he set out again for the giant's castle. Pleased to see him, the giantess invited Jack in for refreshments and again hurried to hide him in the copper pot when the giant came stomping through the door.

"Fee, Fi, Fo, Fum, I smell the blood of an Englishman. Be he alive or be he dead, I'll grind his bones to make my bread," sang the giant as he walked around, sniffing and snuffing, peeping and prying into all the corners and nooks where someone might be hiding. Yet again, his wife sat his dinner on the table and the giant decided that it was his dinner he smelled.

The giant called to his wife to bring him his magic harp, which played wonderful music of its own accord. Listening to the beautiful music, he and his wife soon fell fast asleep. Jack crept very quietly and caught hold of the wonderful harp. But it was an enchanted harp, and when Jack picked it up it loudly called out, "Master, master, wake up!" And the giant did.

"Fee, Fi, Fo, Fum! I smell the blood of an Englishman. If he's alive and not yet dead, I'll grind his bones to make my bread," shouted the giant as he rushed after Jack with his dreadful club in his hand. Jack came to the beanstalk and clambered down as quickly as he could. When he got to the bottom, he felt the stalk

swaying. Looking up, he saw the fierce giant coming down after him. Jack called out to his mother to bring a hatchet. With a few quick strokes, he cut the beanstalk off at the roots. It came tumbling down, and the giant crashed to the earth and lay dead as a stone.

Just then the fairy appeared. She thanked Jack for keeping his promise and told him always to follow his father's example as a kind and generous man. Jack kept his word, and he, his mother, and all those he helped lived happily ever after for a great many years.

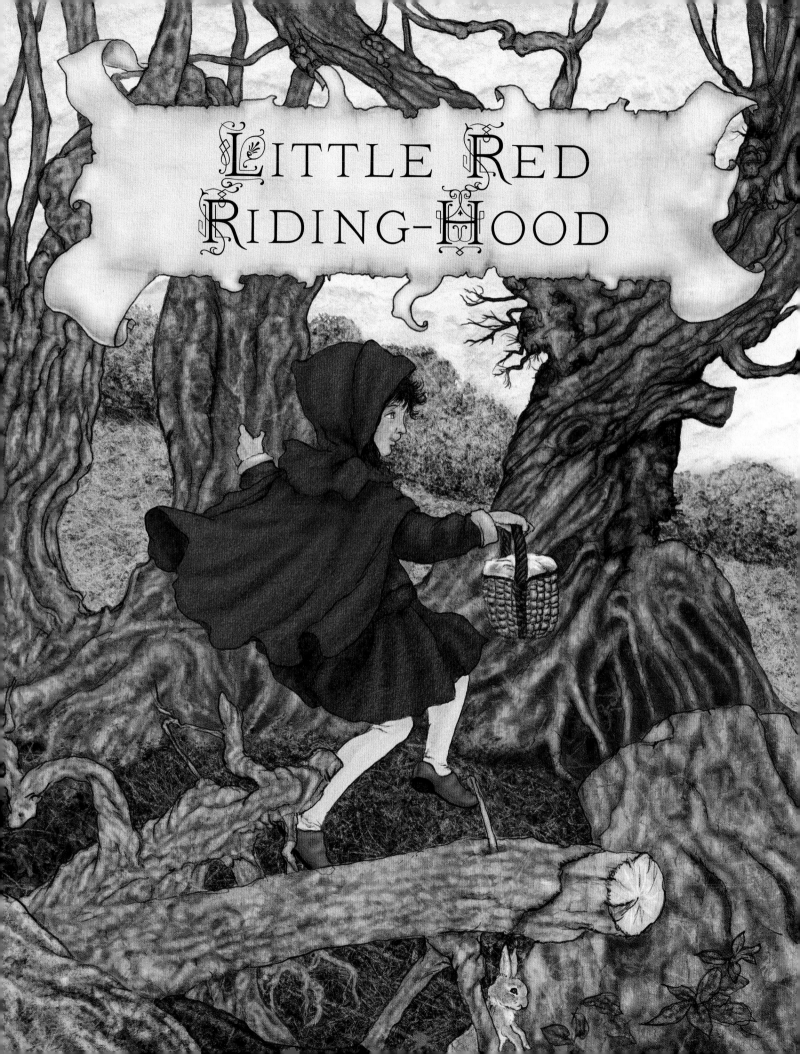

Little Red Riding-Hood

Once upon a time, in a cottage near a wood, there lived a cheerful little girl. Her grandmother, who lived on the other side of the wood, had made a beautiful red cape and hood for her, and everybody called her Red Riding-Hood.

One day Red Riding-Hood's mother said, "Your grandmother has been ill, so I want you to take her some nice fresh bread and jam and see if she is better."

Little Red Riding-Hood packed a basket filled with fresh bread and jam and immediately set out to visit her grandmother. Her mother called out to her as she left, "Stay on the path! Do not play along the way, and do not talk to strangers."

But Little Red Riding-Hood decided to cut through the wood so that she could gather a bouquet of wildflowers for her grandmother. In the wood she met an old wolf. Now, this wolf wanted to eat her up, but he was afraid to do so because of some woodcutters at work nearby. He asked her where she was going, and when she told him, he ran off as fast as he could toward the grandmother's house. He planned to have a meal of the grandmother, wait for Red Riding-Hood, and then eat her up as well. Little Red Riding-Hood, finding it very pleasant in the wood, dawdled along, picking wildflowers and chasing butterflies.

58

Meanwhile, the wolf had reached the grandmother's house and knocked gently on the door.

"Who is there?" asked a voice.

The wolf spoke in a tiny voice, pretending to be Little Red Riding-Hood, "It is I, Little Red Riding-Hood. I have brought you a basket of fresh bread, jam that mother has made, and flowers I picked for you in the wood."

Hearing that, the grandmother, who was ill in bed called out, "Pull the latch and come inside."

The wolf did as she said. He rushed into the room and chased the poor woman around the bed. The grandmother took refuge in a closet and held the door tight to keep the old wolf out.

Just then, the wolf heard a tapping at the door. The old wolf climbed into the grandmother's bed, hiding himself underneath the blankets. He put on the grandmother's nightcap and nightgown and called out, making his voice as soft as possible, "Who is there?"

"It is I, Little Red Riding-Hood. I have brought you a basket of fresh bread, jam that mother has made, and flowers I picked for you in the wood."

"Pull the latch and come inside," replied the wolf.

When Little Red Riding-Hood came into the room, the wolf, trying to speak in a feeble voice said, "Put the basket on the table and come sit and visit with your poor sick grandmother."

So Little Red Riding-Hood sat down. But when she saw how strange her grandmother looked, she said, "Oh, Grandmother, what big arms you have!"

"All the better to hug you with, my dear," answered the wolf.

"Oh, Grandmother, what big ears you have!"

"All the better to hear you with, my dear."

"Oh, Grandmother, what big eyes you have!"

"All the better to see you with, my dear."

Little Red Riding-Hood looked closer and then said, "Oh, Grandmother, what big teeth you have!"

"All the better to eat you with!" said the wolf, and he sprang from the bed and seized the little girl.

At that moment a woodcutter who was working nearby heard Red Riding-Hood's screams and quickly ran into the house, where he chased the wicked wolf into the wood.

Soon the woodcutter returned and joined Little Red Riding-Hood and her grandmother for a slice of fresh bread and jam. Little Red Riding-Hood kissed her grandmother good-bye, and the woodcutter carried Little Red Riding-Hood safely home, singing:

"A little girl
Must keep in mind
What her mother's told her;
A little girl
Must wisdom find
By the time that she is older."

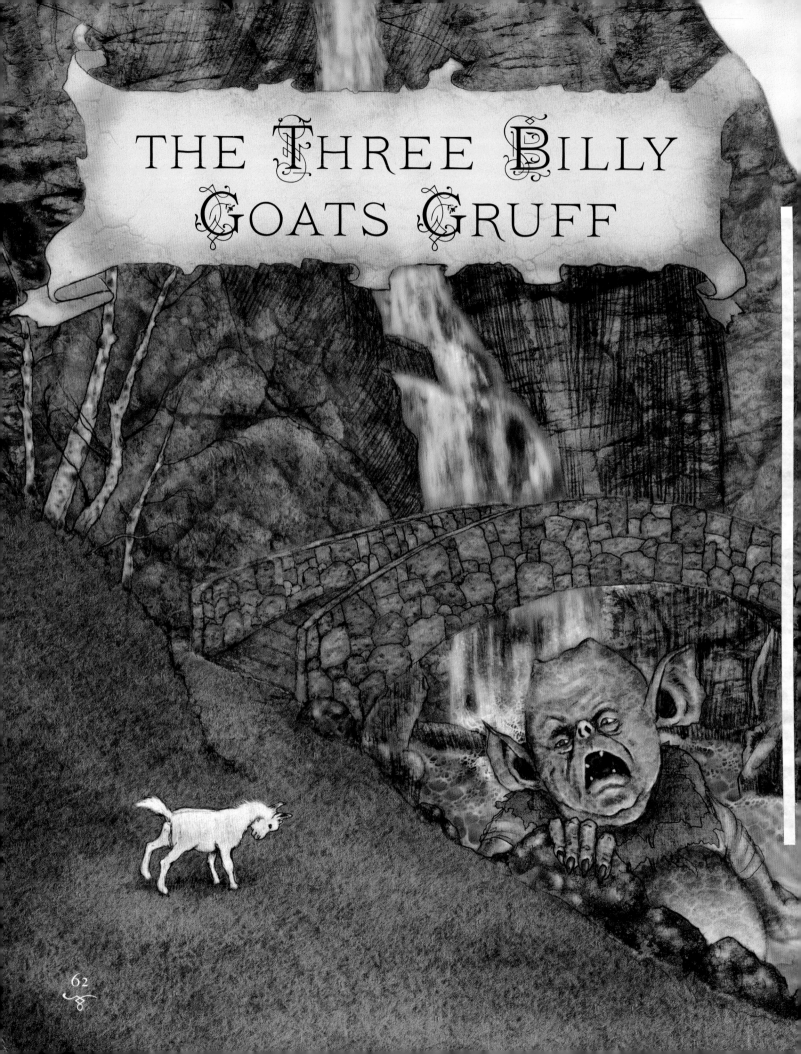

THE THREE BILLY GOATS GRUFF

Once there was a family of three billy goats called Gruff. The billy goats wanted to go up the hillside to the high meadow, where the greenest grass grew. To get to the meadow they had to cross a bridge, and under this bridge lived a large troll. He was as horrible and ugly as he was large.

First across the bridge was the smallest billy goat Gruff. *Trip, trip, trip, trip* echoed his hooves on the bridge.

"Who is tripping over my bridge?" roared the troll.

"It is only I, the smallest billy goat Gruff. I am going to the meadow to make myself fat for the winter," he said.

"I am coming to gobble you up!" growled the troll.

"Oh no! Don't eat me. I am far too small to make a good meal for such a large and hungry troll. Wait until the second billy goat Gruff comes. He is much bigger than I," said the billy goat.

"Very well, then, be off with you," snarled the troll. And the smallest billy goat Gruff ran across the bridge to the meadow.

Next across the bridge was the second billy goat Gruff. *Tramp, tramp, tramp, tramp* echoed his hooves on the bridge.

"Who is tramping over my bridge?" roared the troll.

"It is only I, the second billy goat Gruff. I am going to the meadow to make myself fat for the winter," he said.

"I am coming to gobble you up!" growled the troll.

"Oh no! Don't eat me. I am not big enough to make a good meal for such a large and hungry troll. Wait until the biggest billy goat Gruff comes. He is much bigger than I," said the billy goat.

"Very well, then, be off with you," snarled the troll. And the second billy goat Gruff ran across the bridge to the meadow.

Finally, across the bridge came the biggest billy goat Gruff. *Stomp, stomp, stomp, stomp* echoed his hooves on the bridge.

"Who is stomping over my bridge?" roared the troll.

"It is I, the biggest billy goat Gruff. I am going to the meadow to make myself fat for the winter," he said.

"I am coming to gobble you up!" growled the troll.

"Well, come and stop me if you can," replied the biggest billy goat Gruff.

The troll crawled out from beneath the bridge and flew at the biggest billy goat Gruff. The goat rammed the troll with his big horns and tossed him off the bridge; the troll disappeared into the swirling waters below. After that, the biggest billy goat Gruff crossed the bridge to the meadow. There, the three billy goats Gruff got so fat that they were barely able to run home again.

Trip, tramp, stomp, they run. Now, you see, this tale is done.

THE GINGERBREAD MAN

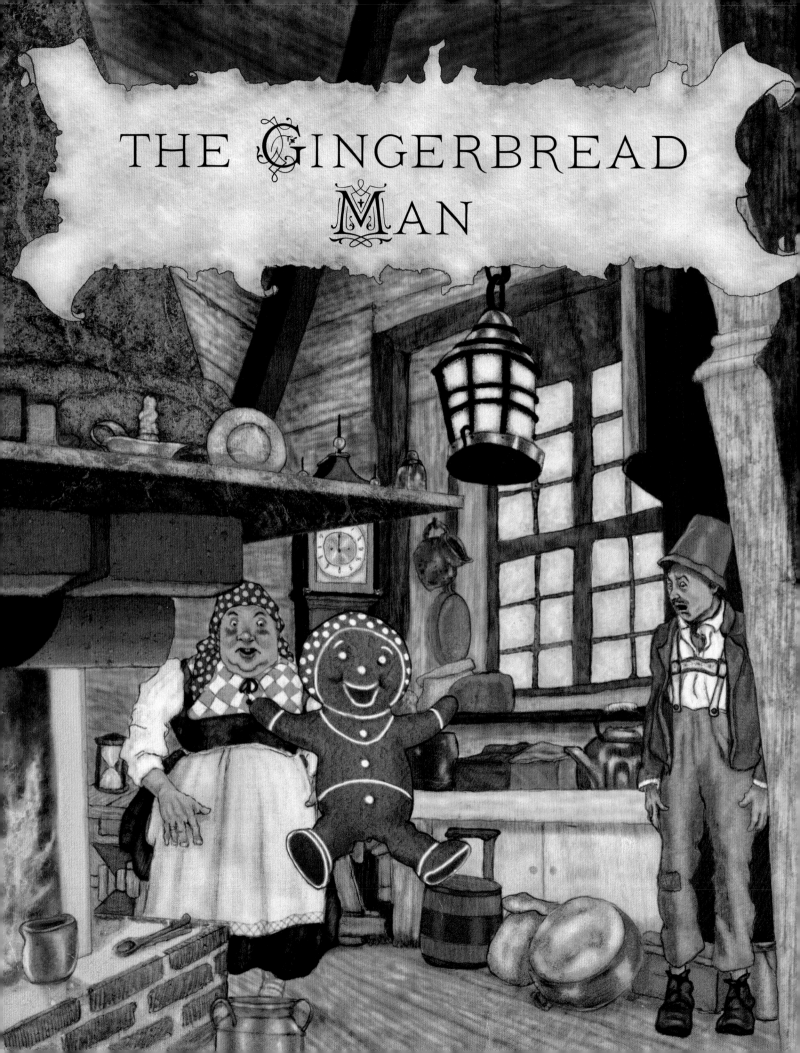

Once upon a time there was a little old woman and a little old man who lived in a little old house. One day, they decided to make a gingerbread man. The little old woman rolled out the gingerbread and pinched him into shape. Then they put the gingerbread man in the oven to bake.

The little old woman and the little old man were very hungry and could hardly wait for the gingerbread man to finish baking. In fact, they couldn't wait, they decided to peek. Imagine their surprise when they opened the oven and the gingerbread man hopped out and ran out the door!

"Stop! Stop!" yelled the little old woman and the little old man as they ran after him. But the gingerbread man did not stop. He ran on, laughing and shouting, "Run, run as fast as you can! You can't catch me, I'm the Gingerbread Man!"

It was not long before the gingerbread man met a cat. "Stop!" meowed the cat. But the gingerbread man did not stop. He ran on, laughing and shouting, "Run, run as fast as you can! You can't catch me, I'm the Gingerbread Man!" And so, the cat joined the little old woman and the little old man in the chase.

A little farther on the gingerbread man met a policeman. "Stop!" commanded the policeman. But the gingerbread man did not stop. He ran on, laughing and shouting, "Run, run as fast as you can! You can't catch me, I'm the Gingerbread Man!" And so, the policeman joined the cat and the little old woman and the little old man in the chase.

The gingerbread man sped down the street until he met a dog. "Stop!" growled the dog. But the gingerbread man did not stop. He ran on, laughing and shouting, "Run, run as fast as you can! You can't catch me, I'm the Gingerbread Man!" And so, the dog joined the

policeman, the cat, and the little old woman and the little old man in the chase.

The gingerbread man ran across a playground where he met three children. "Stop!" shouted the children. But the gingerbread man did not stop. He ran on, laughing and shouting, "Run, run as fast as you can! You can't catch me, I'm the Gingerbread Man!" And so, the children joined the dog, the policeman, the cat, and the little old woman and the little old man in the chase.

Soon the Gingerbread Man met a duck. "Stop!" quacked the duck. But the gingerbread man did not stop. He ran on, laughing and shouting, "Run, run as fast as you can! You can't catch me, I'm the Gingerbread Man!" And so, the duck joined the children, the dog, the policeman, the cat, and the little old woman and the little old man in the chase.

Next the gingerbread man met a gardener. "Stop!" called the gardener. But the gingerbread man did not stop. He ran on, laughing and shouting, "Run, run as fast as you can! You can't catch me, I'm the Gingerbread Man!" And so, the gardener joined the duck, the children, the dog, the policeman, the cat, and the little old woman and the little old man in the chase.

On the gingerbread man ran, until he met a pig. "Stop!" grunted the pig. But the gingerbread man did not stop. He ran on, laughing and shouting, "Run, run as fast as you can! You can't catch me, I'm the Gingerbread Man!" And so, the pig joined the gardener, the duck, the children, the dog, the policeman, the cat, and the little old woman and the little old man in the chase.

The gingerbread man raced across a field until he met a cow. "Stop!" mooed the cow. But the gingerbread man did not stop. He ran on, laughing and shouting, "Run, run as fast as you can! You can't catch me, I'm the Gingerbread Man!" And so, the cow joined the pig, the gardener, the duck, the children, the dog, the policeman, the cat, and the little old woman and the little old man in the chase.

Before too long the gingerbread man came to a river. "Oh no!" he cried. "They will catch me if I cannot get across the river!"

Just then, a sly fox appeared from behind a tree. "I can help you cross the river," said the fox. "Jump on my tail, and I will take you across."

"You won't eat me, will you?" asked the gingerbread man.

"Of course not," said the fox.

The gingerbread man climbed onto the fox's tail, and the fox swam into the river. When the fox had gone a little way from the shore, he turned his head to the gingerbread man and said, "You are too heavy on my tail; I am afraid you will get wet. Jump onto my back." And so, the gingerbread man jumped onto the fox's back.

In the middle of the river, the fox said, "Oh, my back is sinking. Hurry, jump onto my shoulders so you will not get wet." And so, the gingerbread man jumped onto the fox's shoulders.

Near the shore the fox once again turned and said, "You are very heavy and I am tired. Jump onto my nose so I can lift you to the shore." And so, the gingerbread man jumped onto the sly fox's nose.

No sooner had he done so than the fox
threw back his head, tossing the gingerbread
man into the air, and snap!

"Dear me!" shouted the gingerbread man.
"I'm a quarter gone."

Another snap! "Oh no. I am half gone!"
exclaimed the gingerbread man.

And another snap! The gingerbread man cried
out, "I am three-quarters gone!"

With one final snap the sly fox smiled, and the
gingerbread man never said anything more at all.

THE TORTOISE AND THE HARE

Once upon a time there was a boastful hare. Every day he bragged to the other animals that he could run faster than anyone else.

One day the tortoise, annoyed by such bragging, answered back, "Who do you think you are? There's no denying you're swift, but even you can be beaten!"

The hare squealed with laughter. "Beaten? In a race? By whom?" asked the hare. "Not you, surely. There is no one as slow as you! I challenge anyone here to race with me."

The tortoise said, "I accept your challenge."

"That is a good joke!" said the hare.

"Keep your boasting till you've beaten me," answered the tortoise.

A course was agreed upon, and the next day at dawn the tortoise and the hare stood at the starting line. The fox signaled for the race to begin. While the meek tortoise lumbered slowly off, the hare sprinted forward and was soon out of sight.

79

After he had run a ways, the hare stopped. Looking back, he saw how far ahead he was from his slow rival, and he decided there was no harm in taking a quick nap.

The hare woke with a start from his nap but, gazing around, he discovered the tortoise had traveled only a short distance. The hare laughed and decided he might as well have breakfast too. Off he went to munch some cabbages he had noticed in a nearby field.

The heavy meal and the hot sun made his eyelids droop. With a careless glance at the tortoise, now halfway along the course, the hare decided to have another snooze before completing the race. Smiling at the thought of the animals' faces when they saw the hare speed across the finish line, he fell fast asleep and was soon snoring.

The sun started to sink below the horizon, and the tortoise, who had been plodding toward the winning line since morning, was scarcely a yard from the finish. At that very moment, the hare woke with a jolt. He could see the tortoise a speck in the distance, and away he dashed.

Just a little more and the hare would be first at the finish. But his last leap was just too late, for the tortoise had beaten him to the winning post. Poor hare! Embarrassed, he slumped down beside the tortoise, who was smiling.

Slow and steady does it every time!

THE THREE LITTLE PIGS

here were once three little pigs who lived their young lives with their mother and father. Two of the little pigs were very lazy, while the third was hard working. When the three little pigs were old enough to care for themselves, they bid their parents good-bye and left to seek their fortunes in the world.

The first lazy little pig had not gone very far when he stopped at the side of the road to rest. He saw a man approaching, carrying a bale of straw.

"Ah," thought the lazy little pig. "A house of straw will be an easy thing for me to build." So he asked the man, "Please, sir, will you give me that bale of straw to build a house?"

The kind man took pity on the little pig and gave him the bale of straw, and soon the little pig had completed his house.

The second lazy little pig had not gone very much farther when he too stopped at the side of the road to rest. He saw a man approaching, carrying a bundle of sticks.

"Ah," thought the lazy little pig. "A house of sticks will be an easy thing for me to build." So he asked the man, "Please, sir, will you give me that bundle of sticks to build a house?"

The kind man took pity on the little pig and gave him the bundle of sticks, and soon the little pig had completed his house.

The third little pig continued on his journey. He met a man pushing a wheelbarrow of bricks.

"Please, sir," he asked the man. "Will you give me work so that I may buy that wheelbarrow of bricks to build myself a house?"

The kind man gave him work, and the little pig bought the wheelbarrow of bricks. The little pig worked hard, and several days later he had completed his house.

One day a hungry wolf was walking by the straw house. He smelled the little pig and knocked on the door calling, "Little pig, little pig, let me in."

But the little pig peeped through the window and saw the wolf's ears and replied, "No, not by the hair on my chinny-chin-chin!"

"Then," said the wolf, "I'll huff and I'll puff and I'll blow your house in!" So he huffed and he puffed until he blew the house in. The little pig barely escaped and ran to the house of the second little pig.

It wasn't long before the hungry wolf arrived at the second little pig's house of sticks. He smelled the little pigs and knocked on the door calling, "Little pigs, little pigs, let me in."

But the little pigs saw the wolf's paws from under the door and replied, "No, not by the hairs on our chinny-chin-chins!"

"Then," said the wolf, "I'll huff and I'll puff and I'll blow your house in!" So he huffed and he puffed until he blew the house in. The little pigs barely escaped and ran to the house of the third little pig.

By and by the hungry wolf came to the third little pig's house of bricks. He smelled the little pigs and knocked on the door, calling, "Little pigs, little pigs, let me in."

But the little pigs recognized the wolf's voice and replied, "No, not by the hairs on our chinny-chin-chins!"

"Then," said the wolf, "I'll huff and I'll puff and I'll blow your house in!" So he huffed and he puffed and he huffed and he puffed and he huffed and he puffed but he could not blow the brick house in. When he saw that after all his huffing and puffing the house stood firm, he called out, "Little pigs, little pigs, let's be friends. I can tell you where there are some nice turnips."

"Where?" called the little pigs suspiciously.

"In the field at the top of the lane," replied the cunning wolf. "And if you will be ready at six o'clock tomorrow morning, I will show you the way and together we will get some for dinner."

"Yes, we will be ready," said the little pigs.

The next morning the three little pigs got up at five o'clock and ran quickly to the field at the top of the lane. Together they gathered the turnips and returned home.

At six o'clock the wolf arrived at the brick house and knocked on the door calling, "Little pigs, little pigs, I am waiting for you."

"Please don't wait for us," replied the three little pigs, "for we have already been to the field and come back with turnips for our dinner."

When the hungry wolf heard this he was very angry, but he made his voice smooth and gentle and said, "Little pigs, little pigs, I know where there are some nice ripe apples."

"Where?" asked the little pigs without opening the door.

"On a tree at the bottom of the lane," replied the wolf. "And if you will be ready at five o'clock tomorrow morning, I will take you there and we can pick some for dinner."

"Yes, we will be ready," said the little pigs.

The next morning the three little pigs got up at four o'clock and hurried to the bottom of the lane. They climbed the apple tree and picked a basket of nice apples. They were just about to jump down and hurry home with the apples when they saw the wolf coming. The wolf stood at the foot of the tree, looking up at the little pigs. He grinned, showing all of his big, sharp teeth.

"Little pigs, little pigs, why didn't you wait for me?" asked the wolf.

"We were so hungry that we could not wait," replied the little pigs. "Let's share the apples. You can taste and see how nice they are." Then the three little pigs threw all the apples so fast and so hard at the wolf that he could not catch them as they jumped down from the tree. By

the time the wolf reached the brick house, the three little pigs were safely inside. The hungry wolf was furious and pounded on the door calling, "Little pigs, little pigs, you won't escape me this time. I'll climb down the chimney and make a meal of you three right now!" And so the wolf began to scramble up the brick walls onto the roof.

But while the wolf was climbing, the three little pigs stirred the fire in the fireplace into a roaring blaze, where a large pot full of water hung over the flame. When they heard the wolf in the chimney they lifted the lid off the pot, and the wolf tumbled into the boiling water with a splash. The three little pigs covered the pot, and that was the end of the wolf.

The three little pigs rebuilt the houses of the first and second little pigs, but this time they worked hard and bought bricks to build them. And from that day on, the three little pigs lived happily ever after.

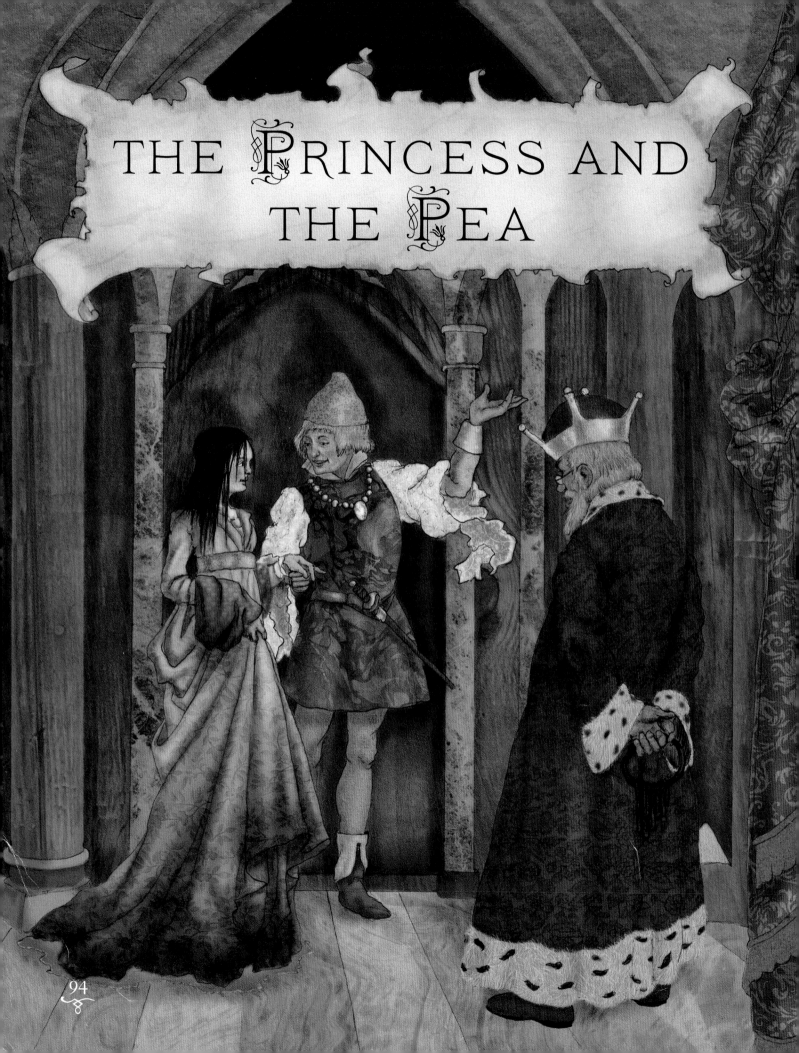

THE PRINCESS AND THE PEA

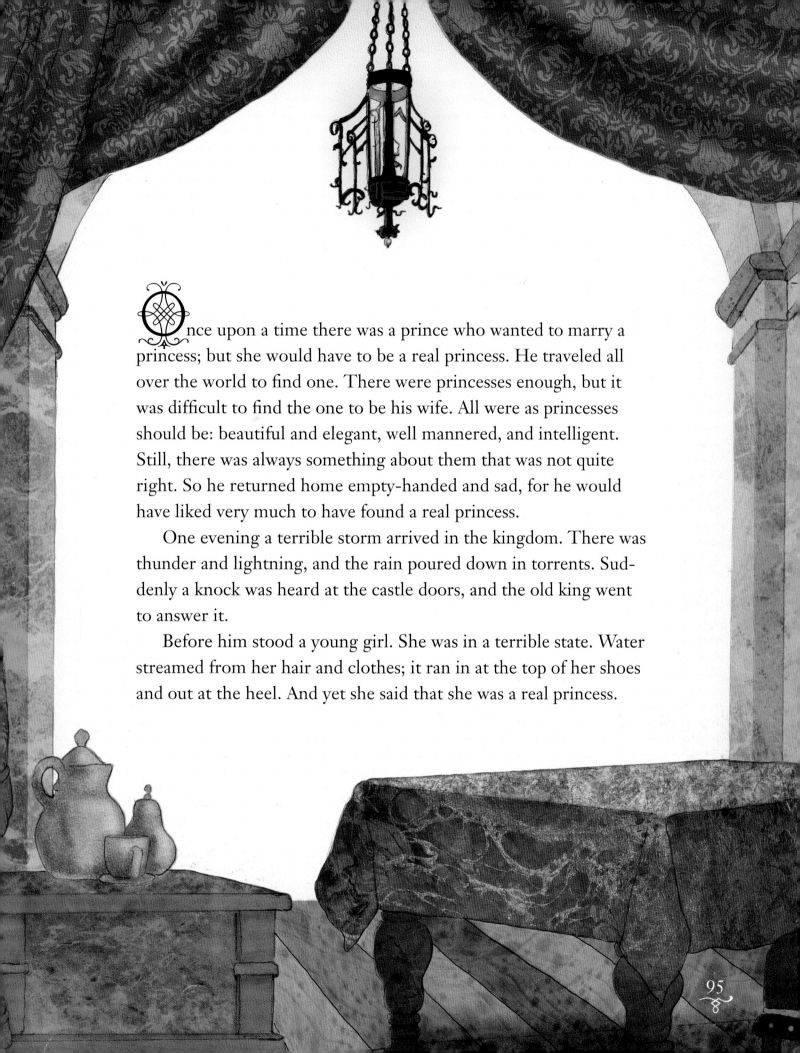

Once upon a time there was a prince who wanted to marry a princess; but she would have to be a real princess. He traveled all over the world to find one. There were princesses enough, but it was difficult to find the one to be his wife. All were as princesses should be: beautiful and elegant, well mannered, and intelligent. Still, there was always something about them that was not quite right. So he returned home empty-handed and sad, for he would have liked very much to have found a real princess.

One evening a terrible storm arrived in the kingdom. There was thunder and lightning, and the rain poured down in torrents. Suddenly a knock was heard at the castle doors, and the old king went to answer it.

Before him stood a young girl. She was in a terrible state. Water streamed from her hair and clothes; it ran in at the top of her shoes and out at the heel. And yet she said that she was a real princess.

"Well, we'll soon find that out," said the queen to the king. "If she is a true princess, she will be sensitive enough to feel this pea." And she held between her thumb and forefinger a small green pea.

The queen went into the guest bedroom, took all the bedding off the bedstead, and placed the pea on the bottom. Then she took twenty mattresses and laid them on the pea, and then she put twenty eiderdown beds on top of the mattresses.

The princess was led to the bedroom, where she climbed a ladder to reach the top of the bed.

"Sleep well," said the queen.

In the morning the queen and king and prince greeted the girl.

"How did you sleep?" asked the queen.

"Oh, terribly badly!" answered the girl. "I scarcely closed my eyes all night. Heaven only knows what was in the bed, but I was lying on something hard, so that I am black and blue all over my body. It's horrible!"

Now they knew she was a real princess because she had felt the pea right through the twenty mattresses and the twenty eiderdown beds.

Nobody but a real princess could be as sensitive as that.

So the prince took her for his wife. And the pea was put in the museum, where it may still be seen today.

THE UGLY DUCKLING

It was summertime. The sunshine fell warmly on an old house. From the house to the water's edge was a place wild and unfrequented. The fields and meadows were skirted by thick woods, and a lake lay in its midst. There, a duck had chosen to make her nest.

At last her eggs began to hatch. One little head after another peered forth from its eggshell.

"How large the world is!" said the little ducklings, gazing at the green leaves surrounding the nest.

"Ah, my little ducklings, this is not the whole of the world," answered the mother duck. "It extends far beyond what you can see." Then the mother duck stood up. "Oh!" she said. "I have not got all of you yet; the largest egg is still here."

When the largest egg hatched at last, out tumbled a duckling not at all like the others. "My," thought the mother duck, "how large and ugly it is."

The next day there was delightful weather, and the sun was shining joyfully when the mother duck led her family down to the lake. Splash! She went into the water. "Quack, quack!" she called, and one duckling after another jumped in. The water closed over their heads, but they all bobbed up again and swam quite easily. All were there; even the ugly gray one swam about with the rest.

"Quack, quack!" said the mother duck. "Now come with me, and I will take you into the world and introduce you to our neighbors. But keep close to me—you are still small and must beware of dangers such as cats." The ducklings followed their mother, walking with their feet turned out and their legs far apart as they had been taught. Soon they met another brood. "How ugly that one is!" cried one of the old ducks and immediately flew at the ugly duckling and bit him on the neck.

"Leave him alone!" scolded the mother duck. "He is doing no one any harm."

"Oh, but he is so large and ungainly," replied the other duck.

"Certainly he is not handsome," said the mother duck, "but he is a very good child. He swims as well as the others—indeed better.

In time he will grow to be like the rest." She stroked the ugly duckling's neck and smoothed his ruffled feathers.

Matters grew worse for the ugly duckling. Even his brothers and sisters behaved unkindly, chasing him and shouting, "May the cat eat you, you hideous thing!" The ugly duckling ran and hid in the hedges. Finally, the ugly duckling decided to run away. He came to a wide moor where some wild ducks lived. He lay there the whole night, feeling sad and alone. In the morning the wild ducks approached. "You are really very ugly," said the wild ducks. So the duckling went away.

Autumn arrived. The leaves turned yellow and brown, and the wind caught them and danced them all about. Winter turned the air cold; the clouds were heavy with sleet and snow. The poor duckling had to swim round and round in the water to keep it from freezing. But every night as the ice thickened, the opening in which he swam became smaller and smaller. At last the weary duckling's legs gave out and he became caught, stiff and cold, in the ice.

Early the next morning a peasant spotted the poor duckling. She broke the ice, carried him home, and placed him in a barn.

It would be a tale too sad to tell if the duckling had not had the safety of the barn to protect him from the ice and snowstorms of the winter. But slowly he revived, and one day as he was lying, his head curled under his wing, he heard larks sing. The sun shone warmly again; beautiful spring had returned.

The ugly duckling shook his wings. They were much stronger than before. He walked through the garden where apple trees were in full bloom, and their fragrance followed him down to the water, where the ice was now gone. Everything was so lovely, so full of the freshness of spring. Suddenly, out of the thicket came three beautiful swans. The ugly duckling saw the glorious creatures and was seized with fear and sorrow. He bowed his head low, ashamed of his ugliness. But as he did, what did he see in the water?

He saw his own reflection, no longer that of a large, ugly, gray duckling—it was that of a swan! He shook his feathers, stretched his slender neck, and in the joy of his heart said, "How little did I dream of so much happiness when I was the ugly duckling!" The larger swans swam round him and stroked him with their beaks, and he was very happy.

He remembered how he had been teased and cruelly treated, and now he was the most beautiful of all beautiful birds.

It matters not to have been born in a duck nest if one has been hatched from a swan's egg.

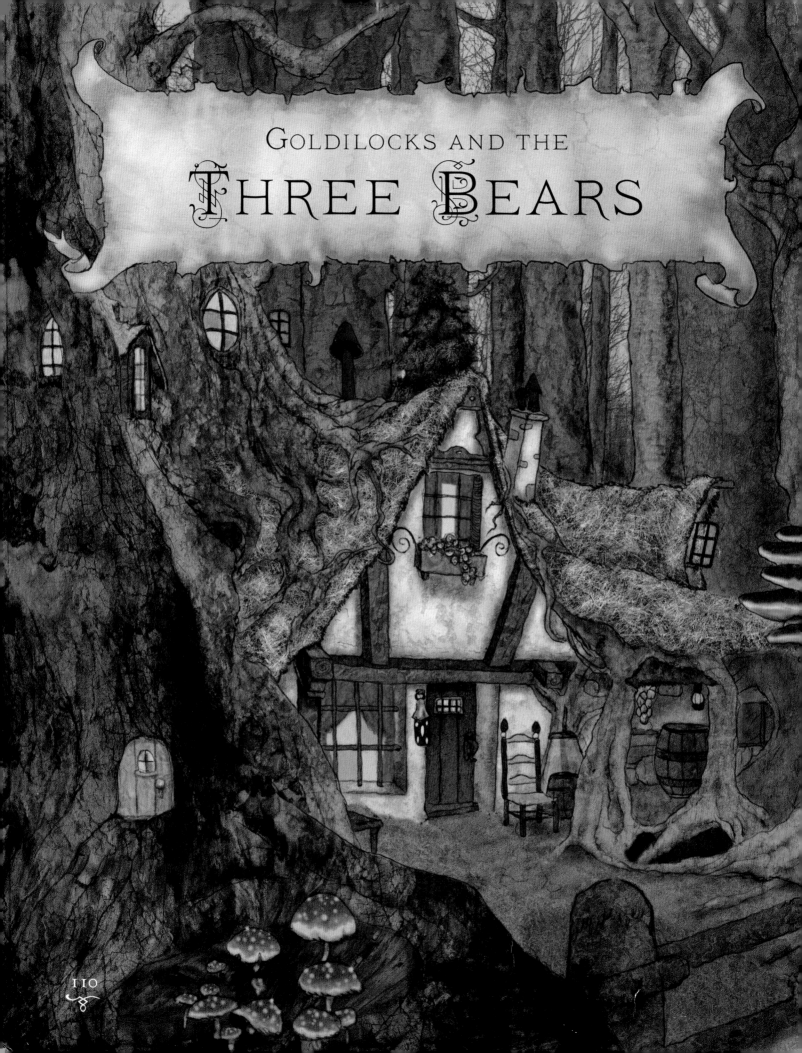

Goldilocks and the
Three Bears

On the top of a hill in the middle of the woods was a little house. In this house lived three bears. There was a wee-small bear, a middle-size bear, and a great-big bear. Each morning they made porridge for their breakfast, and while it cooled, it was their custom to take a walk.

One day, while the three bears were on their walk, a little girl called Goldilocks came upon their house. She had taken a morning walk and lost her way in the woods. She first knocked on the door. Hearing no reply, she peeped through the keyhole. Then she looked in the windows. It seemed that no one was home, and because she was tired and hungry, she tried the door handle. The door was not locked, and so she went inside.

In the middle of the room stood a wooden table, and round it were three chairs. On the table were three bowls of porridge with three spoons beside them. One was a great-big spoon; one was a middle-size spoon; and one was a wee-small spoon.

Goldilocks took up the great-big spoon and tasted the porridge in the great-big bowl, but that was too hot. So she took up the middle-size spoon and tasted the porridge in the middle-size bowl, but that was too cold. So she took up the wee-small spoon and tasted the porridge in the wee-small bowl, and it was just right, so she ate it all up.

When Goldilocks had eaten all the porridge in the wee-small bowl, she looked at the chairs that stood round the table. She sat down in the great-big chair. That was too high. So she sat down in the middle-size chair. That was too big. So she sat down in the wee-small chair. It was neither too high nor too big, and she was very comfortable—until the bottom of the chair fell out and she tumbled to the ground.

Looking about, Goldilocks found a staircase. She climbed the stairs slowly. At the top was a door. She pushed open the door and went inside the room, where she found three beds. She was very tired so she tried the great-big bed, but that was too hard. So she tried the middle-size bed, but that was too soft. So she tried the wee-small bed and it was just right. She climbed into the bed, pulled the wee-small blanket up to her neck, and soon she was fast asleep.

By and by the three bears returned home.

When the great-big bear looked into his great-big bowl, he roared out in his great-big voice, "Somebody has been tasting my porridge!"

The middle-size bear looked into her middle-size bowl and roared out in middle-size voice, "Somebody has been tasting my porridge."

Then the wee-small bear looked into the wee-small bowl and called out in his wee-small voice, "Somebody has been tasting my porridge, and they ate it all up."

The great-big bear put down his bowl and looked at his great-big chair. He roared out in his great-big voice, "Somebody has been sitting on my chair."

The middle-size bear looked at her middle-size chair and roared out in her middle-size voice, "Somebody has been sitting on my chair."

Then the wee-small bear looked at his wee-small chair and cried out in his wee-small voice, "Somebody has been sitting on my chair and broken it all to bits!"

The three bears went slowly up the stairs. The great-big bear went first; the middle-size bear followed next; and then came the wee-small bear. At the top of the stair the door was open, and the three bears went into the room where Goldilocks slept.

The great-big bear looked at the crumpled blankets on his great-big bed and roared out in his great-big voice, "Somebody has been sleeping in my bed!"

The middle-size bear looked at the crumpled blankets on her middle-size bed and roared out in her middle-size voice, "Somebody has been sleeping in my bed."

When the wee-small bear looked at his wee-small bed, he found a sleeping Goldilocks with her head upon his wee-small pillow and his wee-small blanket tucked around her chin. He cried out in his wee-small voice, "Somebody has been sleeping in my bed—and here she is!"

Goldilocks awoke and was startled by the sight of the three bears standing by the side of the bed. She sprang out of the wee-small bed and ran down the stairs and before the bears knew what had happened, Goldilocks ran out the door and off through the woods as fast as the wind. Where she went the bears never found out, but they never saw her again.

CINDERELLA

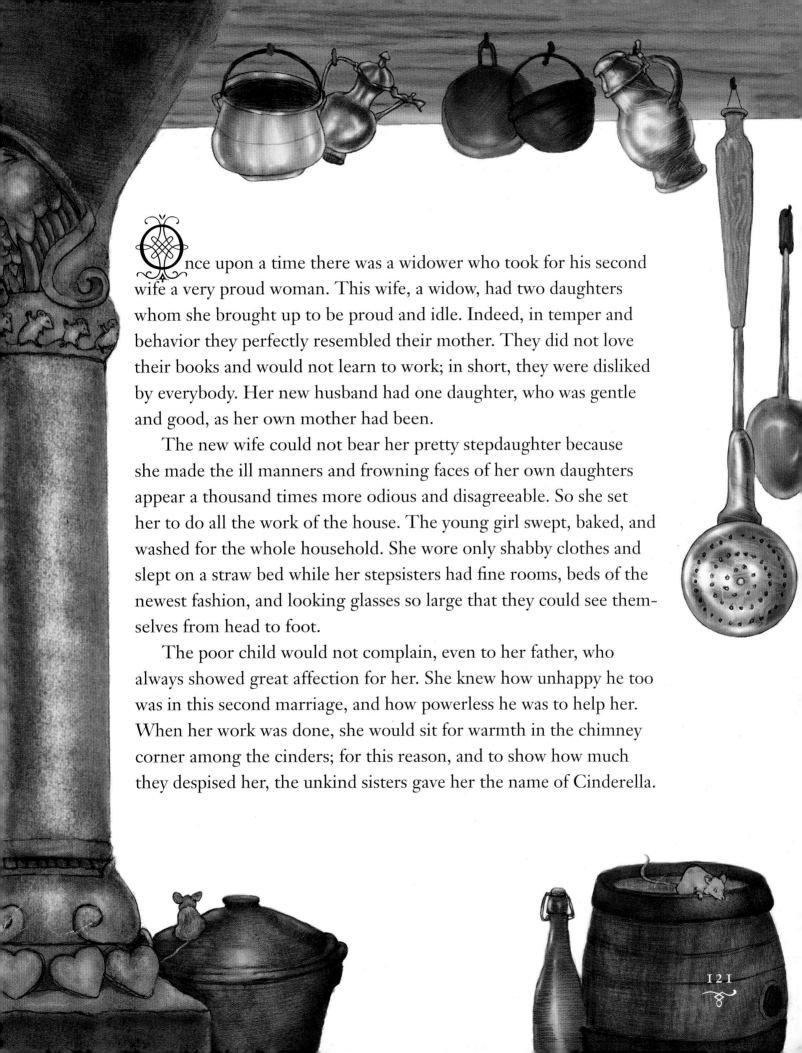

Once upon a time there was a widower who took for his second wife a very proud woman. This wife, a widow, had two daughters whom she brought up to be proud and idle. Indeed, in temper and behavior they perfectly resembled their mother. They did not love their books and would not learn to work; in short, they were disliked by everybody. Her new husband had one daughter, who was gentle and good, as her own mother had been.

The new wife could not bear her pretty stepdaughter because she made the ill manners and frowning faces of her own daughters appear a thousand times more odious and disagreeable. So she set her to do all the work of the house. The young girl swept, baked, and washed for the whole household. She wore only shabby clothes and slept on a straw bed while her stepsisters had fine rooms, beds of the newest fashion, and looking glasses so large that they could see themselves from head to foot.

The poor child would not complain, even to her father, who always showed great affection for her. She knew how unhappy he too was in this second marriage, and how powerless he was to help her. When her work was done, she would sit for warmth in the chimney corner among the cinders; for this reason, and to show how much they despised her, the unkind sisters gave her the name of Cinderella.

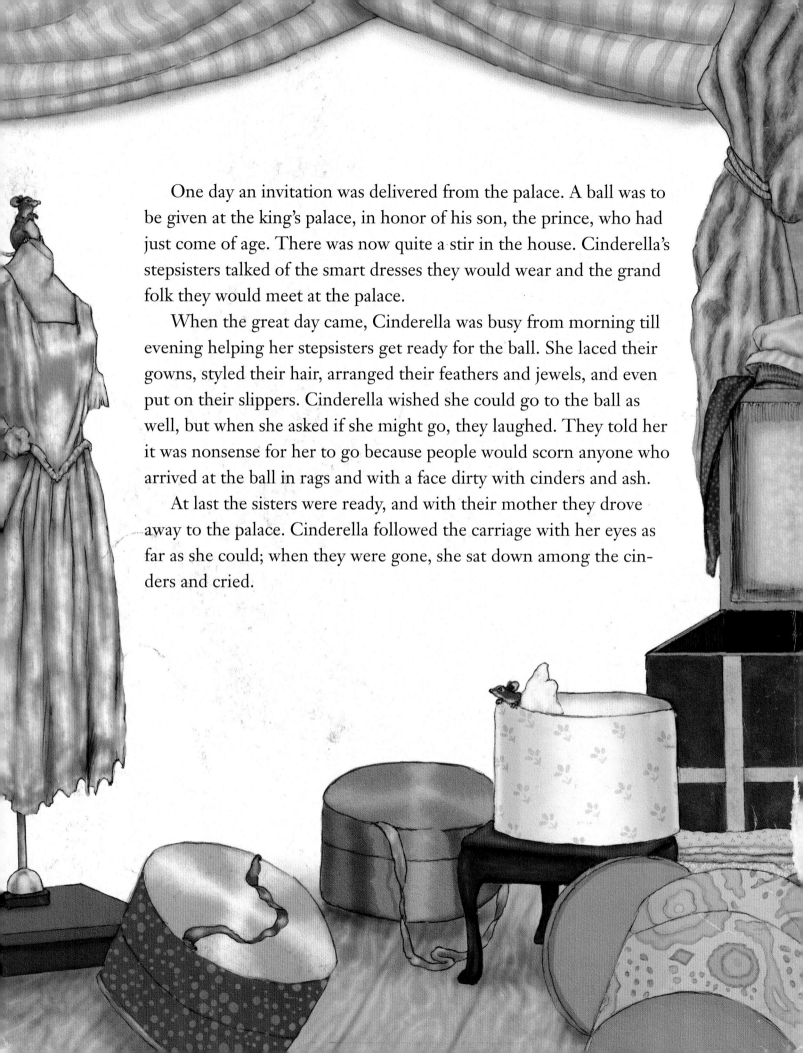

One day an invitation was delivered from the palace. A ball was to be given at the king's palace, in honor of his son, the prince, who had just come of age. There was now quite a stir in the house. Cinderella's stepsisters talked of the smart dresses they would wear and the grand folk they would meet at the palace.

When the great day came, Cinderella was busy from morning till evening helping her stepsisters get ready for the ball. She laced their gowns, styled their hair, arranged their feathers and jewels, and even put on their slippers. Cinderella wished she could go to the ball as well, but when she asked if she might go, they laughed. They told her it was nonsense for her to go because people would scorn anyone who arrived at the ball in rags and with a face dirty with cinders and ash.

At last the sisters were ready, and with their mother they drove away to the palace. Cinderella followed the carriage with her eyes as far as she could; when they were gone, she sat down among the cinders and cried.

Her fairy godmother called out to Cinderella and asked her what was the matter. Cinderella was so surprised to see her that she stopped crying. She told her fairy godmother that she wished to attend the ball at the palace.

Cinderella's fairy godmother told her to run to the garden and fetch the largest pumpkin she could find. Away went Cinderella, and very soon she returned, hugging a big green-and-yellow pumpkin. The fairy godmother scooped out the inside of the pumpkin, leaving nothing but the rind. Then she touched it with her fairy wand, and at once the pumpkin became a fine coach, shining all over with gold, and lined with green.

Then she told Cinderella to bring her a mousetrap. Cinderella obeyed quickly. In the mousetrap were six mice. The fairy god-mother opened the trap, and as each mouse ran out, she touched it with her wand. Each became a mouse-colored, dapple-gray horse to pull the magnificent coach.

Next the fairy godmother told Cinderella to bring her a rattrap. Cinderella brought it at once. There was a large rat inside, and the fairy godmother touched it with her wand. At once the rat became a jolly coachman.

The fairy godmother told Cinderella to bring her the six green lizards that were hiding behind the watering can in the garden.

Cinderella brought the six lizards, and at a touch of the wand, each one was turned into a footman in a smart uniform.

Cinderella gazed in amazement at the beautiful coach, then sadly looked down at her own shabby clothes and stately footmen.

As she did so, Cinderella's fairy godmother touched Cinderella with her wand and instantly her old clothes were turned into robes of silk and velvet, glittering with jewels. On her feet was a little pair of shining glass slippers, the prettiest that ever were seen.

As one of the footmen helped Cinderella into the coach, her fairy godmother told her not to stay one moment after midnight, for at the last stroke of twelve the coach would become a pumpkin again, her horses mice, her coachman a rat, her footmen lizards, and her clothes just as they were. Cinderella promised to do as she was told, and away she drove to the ball.

When Cinderella entered the ball, the musicians ceased playing, the dancers stopped dancing, and all gazed in surprise at the lovely unknown princess. The prince fell in love with her at first sight and would speak to and dance with no other that night. Cinderella was enjoying herself so much that she quite forgot about the time.

Suddenly she heard the clock begin to strike twelve. She fled from the ballroom and, in her haste, lost one of her slippers. The prince ran after Cinderella, but when he reached the palace steps, he could see no sign of the lovely princess—only a little glass slipper lying on the staircase.

The next morning the folk of the kingdom were awakened by the sound of trumpets. The king sent the royal chamberlain out through the streets of the town with guards and an attendant carrying the little glass slipper on a velvet cushion. The king proclaimed that the prince would marry the young lady whose foot fit the glass slipper. Throughout the kingdom all the young ladies tried on the glass slipper. But it would fit none of them; their feet were too big.

At last the chamberlain arrived at Cinderella's house. Both Cinderella's stepsisters were eager to try on the slipper. But, though they pinched their toes and squeezed their heels, their feet were far too large. Then the royal chamberlain inquired whether any other young women were in the house.

Cinderella came shyly out from behind the door where she had been watching. She asked if she could try on the slipper. Her stepmother and stepsisters laughed and told her to return to her cinders. But the chamberlain stopped Cinderella, proclaiming that the king had decreed that every young woman in the kingdom was to try on the glass slipper.

Cinderella sat down. The royal chamberlain tried the slipper on Cinderella's foot—and it fit perfectly! Then, to everyone's surprise, Cinderella drew the matching glass slipper from her pocket and put it on as well. At that moment her fairy godmother appeared, and with a touch of her wand, she changed Cinderella's poor garments into robes more splendid than ever.

Everyone saw that she was indeed the beautiful princess whom the prince loved. Soon Cinderella and the prince were married amid great rejoicing.

As for the ugly stepsisters and their mother, they were so jealous that they turned green with envy. They grew uglier and uglier every day, until at last they became so ugly inside and out that nobody could bear to look at them, and they lived the rest of their days alone and miserable. But the kindness and love that Cinderella showed to all those around her made her more and more beautiful, and she lived happily with the prince forever afterward.